For
Aaron and Sean
and sweet Maureen
– J.L.

For
Wendy "Newt" Boase
with love and thanks
– L.V.

First published 1996 by
Walker Books Ltd
87 Vauxhall Walk
London SE11 5HJ

This edition published 1998

10 9 8 7 6 5 4 3

Text © 1996 Jonathan London
Illustrations © 1996 Louise Voce

This book has been typeset in
Journal Text and Journal Italic.

Printed in Hong Kong

British Library Cataloguing in
Publication Data
A catalogue record for this book is
available from the British Library.

ISBN 0-7445-5493-4

What Newt Could Do for Turtle

Written by
Jonathan London

Illustrated by
Louise Voce

WALKER BOOKS
AND SUBSIDIARIES
LONDON · BOSTON · SYDNEY

Spring had come to the swamp.
A red-spotted newt crawled out
from his winter bed in the mud.
"Help!" cried Newt. "I'm stuck!"
A painted turtle yawned,
greeting the spring.
"Coming, dear Newt!"
cried Turtle.

Pock! went the mud
as Turtle pulled Newt free.
"Thanks, Turtle! You're the best!"

"That's what friends are for!" said Turtle.
"Yep," said Newt.
His spots turned a deeper red,
and he wondered,

What can I do for Turtle?

That spring the swamp buzzed with life.
There were catfish and dragonflies, cat's-tails
and dogwoods, polecats and tadpoles.
Turtle took good care of Newt, and Newt
and Turtle were happy just to be together.
But, sometimes, when Newt sat alone
on his thinking rock, he wondered,
What can I do for Turtle?

In the summer Newt and Turtle
played in their favourite swimming holes.
They *swooshed* down muddy banks and crashed
into the water together – *splash!*

Playing hide-and-seek, Newt
climbed on to Turtle's back.

"*Yoo-hoo!* Turtle!
Where are you?"
He thought he was
on a rock.

"*Boo!*" said Turtle,
poking his head out.
Newt jumped high into the air.

One day a cottonmouth snake slithered off
a branch and whispered through
the water. Snake swam straight
towards Newt.

He was about to strike when
Newt heard Turtle's voice,
"Newt! A snake!"

Newt plunged into the water ...

and hid at the bottom of the swamp.
Once again, Newt wondered,

What can I do for Turtle?

Autumn came and the leaves of the swamp
trees sailed down like little umbrellas.
One day Newt was paddling a leaf when
an alligator glided up to him.

Turtle was watching but he
was so scared he hit the water with
a great *smack!* and went under.
Alligator turned her head to look,
and at that moment Newt dived away.

Newt and Turtle hid together beneath
the duckweed. Newt sighed, happy
to be alive, and his
spots turned redder.
Now, more than ever,
he wondered,
What can I do for Turtle?

Then, one day, a curious bobcat slunk
through the reeds, twitched his whiskers
and *pounced* — right on to Turtle's back.

"*Yikes!*" yelled Turtle,
pulling his head inside his shell.
Bobcat batted with his paws
and flipped Turtle over.
Then he grew bored
and trotted back into the forest.
Poor Turtle wriggled back and forth.
If he could not roll over, he
would dry up and die!

"Newt, oh Newt!" he cried.
"Where are you?"

Now, across the swamp,
Newt was dreaming that
Turtle was in trouble.

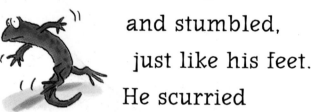

"What can I do for Turtle?"
he said. His
own words
woke him up!
His heart bumped
and stumbled,
just like his feet.

He scurried
to and fro,
searching
for his
friend.

At last, beneath a weeping willow,
Newt found him.
"Turtle!" cried Newt. "What
are you doing?"
"Pretending I'm a bowl of soup.
What does it look like
I'm doing?"
"Don't worry," said Newt.
"I'll help you."

This was his big chance!

Newt went to his thinking rock, and
thought and thought.

"*Aha!*" he said at last.

He hauled a big stick over to Turtle
and stuck it under his shell.

He pushed a rock beneath the stick ...

then he sprang up,
grabbed hold and swung.

"Rock 'n' roll!" cried Newt.

Turtle wobbled, teetered on edge ...
and toppled over.
"Hooray!" shouted Turtle. "You *did* it!"
"That's what friends are for!" sang Newt.
Turtle stretched out his neck and
gently nuzzled Newt. Newt's spots
turned so dark they were almost purple.

The days were getting shorter.
Ducks splashed off, chattering news of winter.
Newt licked a toe and held it up,
testing the breeze. "Yep," he said.
"Winter has finally come."
Turtle nodded with a drowsy smile.
"Well," said Newt, "it's nice knowing what
we can do for each other."
"Yes," said Turtle wisely, "these things
are worth remembering."

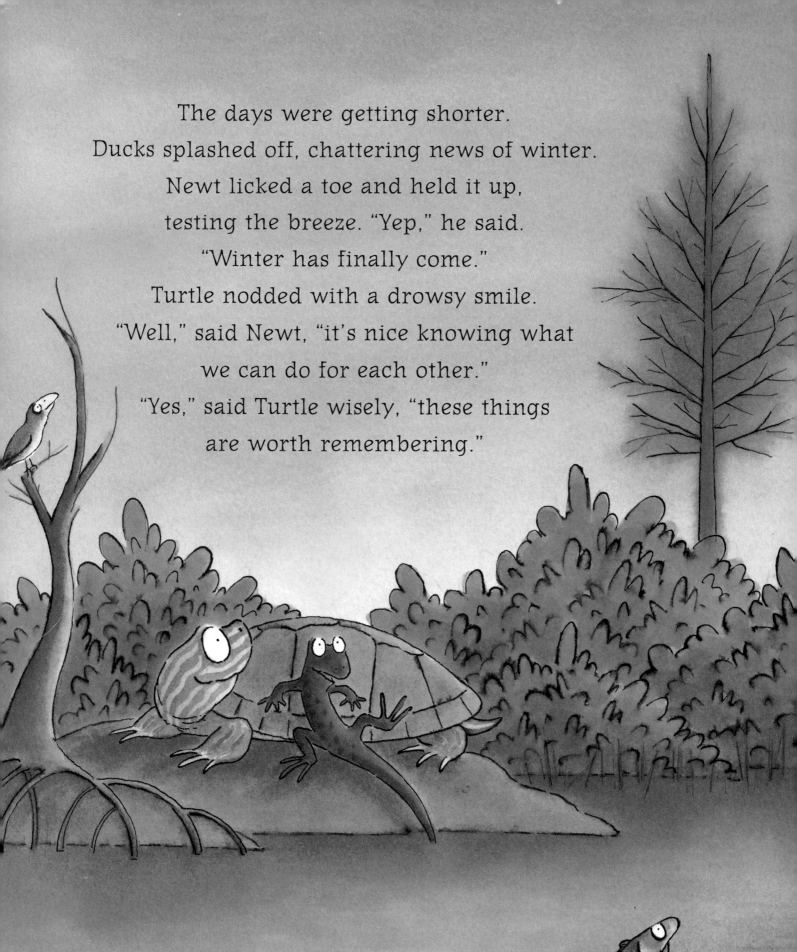

"Goodnight, Turtle," said Newt.
"See you next spring!"
"Goodnight, Newt!" said Turtle.
And they
slipped
deep into
the swamp mud, where it
was snug and cosy and warm.
"Sleep tight!" murmured Turtle.

And that is what they did.
All winter.

MORE WALKER PAPERBACKS
For You to Enjoy

Also illustrated by Louise Voce

HELLO, GOODBYE
by David Lloyd

First there is just a tree. Then a bear comes along, then a bee,
then all sorts of other animals appear – and disappear!

"Wonderful story… Bright, simple illustrations… A good book to use as a reading
aid and great for the young child, too." *Nursery World*

0-7445-1348-0   £4.99

THE OWL AND THE PUSSYCAT
by Edward Lear

"One of the best-loved nonsense rhymes of all time… The simple illustrations have
an appealing charm – a picture book children will love." *Practical Parenting*

0-7445-3121-7   £4.99

OVER IN THE MEADOW
by Louise Voce

"Easy to memorise, counting rhymes allow children the pleasure of joining in,
and are a great boost to the confidence of beginner readers. Louise Voce's
version of *Over in the Meadow* is just the ticket." *The Daily Telegraph*

0-7445-4313-4   £4.99